CAMP KIDS

AND
THE UNDERWATER
ADVENTURE

Stone Fence Publishing

KEEP SWIMMING WITH THE CAMP KIDS IN...

BOOK 2

CAMP KIDS
AND
SERPY'S WILD ADVENTURE

...

BOOK 3

CAMP KIDS
AND
THE TREASURE MAP

CAMP KIDS

AND
THE UNDERWATER
ADVENTURE

WRITTEN & ILLUSTRATED
BY SHARON SWAIN

Cover design by Jonn Griffin and Sharon Swain

Published by:
Stone Fence Publishing
Burnt Hills, NY, 12027
USA

Printed in the United States of America
Second printing 2011
ISBN: 978-0-9827847-0-9
Copyright © 2010 by Stone Fence Publishing

www.stonefencepublishing.com

FOR MY CAMP KIDS,

COLIN AND SOPHIE,
THEIR CAMP FRIENDS JULIANNA AND JACKSON,

AND FOR MY WONDERFUL HUSBAND,

MARK

THANK YOU TO ALL OF MY EDITORS;

GEORGETTE, ABBY, KAREN, KRISTIN AND SUSAN.

THANK YOU JONN FOR ALL YOUR CREATIVE WORK WITH THE COVER
AND THANK YOU TO MILLER PRINTING.

CONTENTS

CHARACTERS

Name: Grace Sophia Galley
Jobs: second grader, little sister to Cole
Interests: reading, writing, drawing, acting
Quote: "Hold on, let me just write that down."

Name: Colin (Cole) Mark Galley
Jobs: fourth grader, big brother to Grace
Interests: soccer, video games, surfing (but I haven't been yet)
Quote: "Awesome. Yep, that about sums it up, awesome."

Name: Julia Anne Morgan
Jobs: second grader, stuffed animal collector, aspiring cook
Interests: anything new and hip
Quote: "Just write the company, tell them they're old news!"

Name: Jacob (Jake) Holden Leftwich, III
Jobs: fourth grader, quarterback
Interests: surfing, football, basketball, golf
Quote: "Dude, just watch me."

CHAPTER 1
SUMMER BEGINS

"I'm going to get there first!" taunted Cole, shaking his shaggy blond hair out of his eyes. He ran off, taking the lead of the group of four kids running up the dirt road.

"No way! I'm going to be the first one this year," hollered Jake, with the tiniest hint of a southern drawl. He jumped over a pile of pine cones and caught up with Cole.

"It doesn't matter who gets there first, it's not like we've figured out how to get inside yet," Julia laughed, adjusting her glasses. "Those two haven't changed at all, have they?" She pushed her bright pink paisley bag higher up on her shoulder and looked up at Grace. Although they were both eight, Julia had always had to look up at Grace, who seemed to grow taller every day. "Does Cole care that you're taller than him?"

Grace pushed a few strands of bright red hair away from her face and smiled. "Nah, he's still my older brother, and he doesn't let me forget it." She smirked as she watched the boys running up the road. "I wonder if this summer will be any different. It starts the same way every year."

"Yeah, except now I have this bag. My grandmother got it for me in Paris. Wait till you see what else she got me," Julia said patting the bag.

Cole and Jake continued the race up the dirt road, leaping over the roots, rocks, and puddles, hooting and hollering the whole way.

It was a familiar scene. These kids racing up to the end of the dirt road, alerting all of the people in the camps along the way that summer had officially begun. It was the same way the kids had started their summer at the small lake in the Adirondacks for as long as they could remember.

Cole and his sister, Grace, would arrive at the lake the last Friday of June every year. They would stay at their camp with their mom and dad until the last Friday in August. Sometimes their dad would have to drive the two hours home to solve some problem with his business, but otherwise both of their parents were at camp, painting, reading, and just taking it easy.

Julia would arrive late that same Friday night. To her utter and complete despair, her father continued to drive the five hours to work each week, so he was only at camp on the weekends. Julia spent most of her week in sheer panic mode, certain that she and her mom would be attacked by a bear or a raccoon.

Once, after watching an Animal Planet show about alligator attacks, she was sure that she saw an alligator lurking in the swampy area at the end of the road. She refused to go to the clubhouse for a whole week, claiming that the alligator had looked at her with hungry eyes. She wrote a letter to the director of the show telling him that they shouldn't air shows about such scary things.

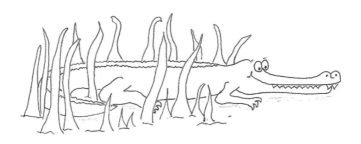

Jake always flew to New York alone, from Southern California. He arrived on the last Saturday of June and stayed the summer with his grandparents at their camp. Ever since his mom had disappeared when he was just one, Jake's dad had insisted that he spend his summers at camp.

Jake loved camp, but he couldn't help being mad about missing the surf competition every year. And his dad spent all of his time at the Oceanography Center anyway, what did he care if Jake was home? Not only that, but since his grandparents had installed the glass observatory overlooking the lake, they hardly ever even left the camp anymore, claiming that they could watch Jake swim and play from inside. As he figured it, he was pretty much on his own either way.

But from the minute Jake stepped out of his grandparents' car that Saturday afternoon, the four kids were inseparable.

"I told you I'd be the first," Cole gloated as he fell to the ground in front of the old abandoned camp that the kids had claimed as their clubhouse. One sandal had fallen off along the way and Cole's foot was now dotted with small spots of sap, each one coated with sand and pine needles.

"But I'm the winner," Jake claimed with a giant smile, "'cause I'm the first to touch the moose. We agreed that was the rule last year. Remember?" He reached for the door of the cabin and touched the wooden cut-out shape of a moose just above the key hole.

"Ugh, I forgot that part. Come on. Let's make a plan for the day."

CHAPTER 2
THE PLAN

Cole picked up his sandal and sat down on a rock that he had unofficially claimed as his seat around the clubhouse fire pit.

"All right, I've got posters and duct tape and music and drinks for everyone," Julia announced, setting down her bag and pushing PLAY.

"Come on Julia, can't you pick some better music? The Smith Brothers, really?" Jake started looking through the posters that she had in a pile ready to tape up on the side of the clubhouse. "And there is no way that we're going to be looking at all these Disney bopper girls all summer, right Cole?" Jake rolled his eyes and looked to Cole for support.

"I forget you don't have a sister, this stuff doesn't even bother me anymore. Actually I kinda like some of them," Cole said as he jumped on Jake and tackled him to the ground, looking extra pale against Jake's dark bronzed skin.

"Jeeze, you're white, Cole, doesn't the sun ever shine where you live?" Jake grunted, pushing Cole off with a burst of energy. "Won again, that makes two to zero! Dude, just three more years till I can teach you to surf and maybe you can even get a tan like this." Jake ran his hand down each arm, like a game show host demonstrating a self-bronzing lotion.

"I know. Every birthday is like a countdown till I'm thirteen," Cole sighed. Jake's dad had promised that he could stay home for the summer when he turned thirteen. He even said he could invite Cole to come and stay for a few weeks.

"Yeah, three more years until we have a peaceful summer. Now that is something to look forward to," Julia chuckled, struggling to pull a big book out of her bag.

"You know, I was thinking," Grace began, watching Julia struggle with the book, "last summer we never really had any adventures, like we always hear our parents talk about. I think this summer we need to do something great."

"Yeah, all right, Nancy Drew, what did you have in mind, a ghost hunt?" Cole never missed a chance to tease his sister. "But you know, you're right, it would be cool to do something new this summer."

"I think it's a great idea. What do we do?" Jake looked at his three camp friends with a spark of mischief in his dark blue eyes. "How about we go diving for that car that everyone is always talking about at the bottom of the lake?"

"Unless you're a trained scuba diver with a wet suit and oxygen tank, I don't think that will be it," Grace said, hand on her hip. She sat down and pulled a journal out of her bag.

Julia stood up. "I know! Why don't we go ring the bell at the church camp?" She adjusted her glasses and bit her lip. "Uh, I've heard tons of stories about the kids in the woods doing that," adjusting her glasses again, "but I'm pretty sure all of those stories end with the kids getting caught. So never mind, I don't think we should do that one."

"Why don't we start with our own adventure? Grace, remember when Grandma took us into the woods and we saw…, well…, oh never mind." Cole's round cheeks turned a little pink.

"Do you mean last summer? Cole, I think that's a great idea." Grace turned to Julia and Jake. "Our grandma showed us this really cool place back in the woods, and you won't believe us, but we saw fairies there." Grace's light amber eyes twinkled. That is until she looked at Cole. "Oh, don't give me that look, Cole, you saw them too."

"I know, but just because you and Grandma and I believed it, it doesn't mean you can go and tell these guys about it." He looked down at his feet, shaking his head back and forth.

"You're being ridiculous Cole. This is Jake and Julia we're talking about here. You believe us, right?" Grace looked at the two friends.

"Ah, yeah, I believe you *think* you saw something, but as the saying goes 'ya gotta see it, ta believe it' and until I see it, I won't believe it," Jake drawled, crossing his arms and waiting to hear what Julia had to say.

Julia grinned at the group. "Well, I hope you can find that spot again, so Jake and I don't have to tell everyone that you guys are seeing things." She giggled as she smoothed down the bottom corner of her favorite poster. "It's better than getting into trouble anyway."

"Come on, let's do it. I'm sure we could find the spot again. It was out in back of our camp, headed toward the big lake. You remember, right, Cole?" Grace said, her voice getting louder.

"Yeah, yeah, I remember. But if we go, these two have to promise to be nice," Cole demanded, sticking both thumbs out, pointing to his two skeptical friends.

"You're on!" Jake began skipping around the fire pit that stood at the center of the circle outside the clubhouse and chanted, "A-fairy hunt'n we'll go!"

"All right, let's get moving so we can be back before it gets too hot. I want to swim all afternoon!" Julia said, lugging the heavy book back into her designer bag.

"Last one there's a rotten lump of cabbage!" Cole yelled. He and Jake both jumped up and began running back down the dirt road toward their camps.

CHAPTER 3
THE WOODS

"Grace, hurry up! You need to lead the way. You're better at this stuff," Cole shouted back to his sister as he did a running jump, landing an inch short of Jake's marker.

"Cole, Jake, slow down!" Grace called back. "I want to write down what we're doing. If we really find the fairy circle, we want to be able to get back here again." Grace had perfected writing and walking at the same time, but in the woods with all the fallen trees and roots, it wasn't easy.

"Okay. Farthest throw gets two points," Cole challenged. "I want to even the score while we wait."

The boys launched their sticks into the air. Jake's caught on one of the many trees. Cole's stick managed to soar right through a group of branches and landed a good ten feet past Jake's.

Cole immediately jumped up and began playing an air guitar. "I think I ought to deliver this in a song. Are you listening?" He began singing his self-made theme song:

I rock, ohhhhh yeah
I rock out loud! Yeah, I rock like a pie
Grandma's apple kind
Yeah, yeah, yeah

Jake just stared at Cole and slowly shook his head from side to side. "Dude, you are so weird sometimes."

"That's tie score, three to three," Cole cheered, watching the girls climb over the huge fallen tree.

"Cole, you remember how Mom and her sisters told us about the fort that they had down here when they were little?" Grace panted, struggling to help Julia. "Julia and I were just talking and I'm sure they said it was called Never, Never Land. Doesn't that mean that maybe they saw fairies too?"

"I used to love that movie. Tinkerbell is so cute." Julia sighed and sat on top of the tree, dropping her bag with a thump. "Can we stop for a snack? I'm tired," she said, pulling fruit snacks out of her bag.

"Awesome. Thanks, Julia." Jake grabbed a packet for himself, not bothering to ask, and climbed onto a huge glacial rock. He looked down at his friends, rubbing his belly and savoring the sweet artificial taste of his treat. "Nothing beats the taste of Red Dye #4. Which way is it now?" He put his hands up to his eyes as binoculars and began singing, "Fairies, fairies, where are youuuuuuu?"

"Ha, Ha, really funny. You promised not to tease." Grace pointed behind her. "It's that way somewhere, down the hill."

Jake continued to scope out the area through his hand binoculars. Then he stopped and leaned forward to get a better look. "Hey, what's that over there? Do you see that little, white thing? It's moving."

"Leth's go thee." Julia struggled to get the words out through the fruit gummies that were now stuck in her teeth, while hefting her bag onto her shoulder.

Grace was the closest and first to reach the area that Jake had pointed to. "It's just some dragonflies. Come see, they're the most amazing colors." Grace held up the golden green dragonfly that had landed on her finger.

"They're cool, but they're no fairies." Jake reached out to the take the dragonfly from Grace, but it flew away fluttering down the hill.

"Follow him. It should be right down the hillside there, heading toward that swamp." Grace led the way down the embankment toward a small clearing, following right behind the dragonfly.

"Do we really have to go to the swamp?" Julia asked, clinging tightly to her bag.

Jake grunted, "We told you last year, there are no alligators in the Adirondacks."

"I know, it's just…ah…well, are you sure?" Julia took her bag in both hands looking like she was ready to throw it.

"Yes, we're sure. You're fine." Grace walked back up the hill and took Julia's arm. "What do you have in that bag anyway?"

"It's a French cookbook that my grandmother got for me. I figured I can read it when I'm bored, and I can also use it as a weapon if a raccoon or bear, or even an alligator tries to attack me."

"Oh. I see. Well stay with me and hopefully you won't have to use it." Grace grinned at Cole and began nudging Julia down the hill.

Cole stopped and bent down to examine a group of trees perched on the hillside. "Look, that's their house, right there under the tree. Remember, Grace?"

CHAPTER 4
FAIRIES

"Do you see it, Grace? I remember that Grandma said they lived in the bottom of that tree, the one with the funny roots." Cole stepped closer to a large tree trunk on the hillside. It had all of its roots exposed, creating a little cave of space underneath. "And look, there's the place where we thought we saw the fairies flying around," he pointed toward a circle of rocks in the clearing.

"You're right. This is it! Come on, let's go see if we can see anything!" Grace shrieked, pulling Julia with her down to the clearing.

"Hey, what's that?" Julia stopped dead in her tracks, yanking Grace back. She pointed toward the circle.

"What? What is it?" Jake asked, eyes darting around.

"That. Don't you see it? Right there in the circle. That light." Julia squeezed Grace's hand a little tighter.

"Yeah, I see it. Is it moving? Do you see it?" Jake turned to Cole and Grace with a look of disbelief.

"Didn't we tell you? Now do you believe us? Just look." Cole stared at the little glimmering light, floating just over the ground, little wings, just visible, fluttering back and forth and twinkling.

"There's another one." Jake pointed toward the edge of the swamp.

"And there," Grace echoed, pointing at the circle of rocks again, where there were now two flickering lights.

"They keep changing colors. Come on. Let's go get a closer look." Jake ran down to the circle. He stopped, leaned forward and slowly turned around with a smug smile on his face. "It's not fairies. It's just those dragonflies again. Come on and see for yourselves."

The rest of the kids reached the circle and bent toward the dragonflies. They were sitting on colorful, sparkling stones.

The stones weren't like any stones that they had ever seen before. And why were those dragonflies hovering over them?

"Hey look, there's another one." Cole bent down to pick up the stone, which was lodged in a knot in the fallen tree. "This thing is so cool. Check it out, you guys."

Each of the kids picked up a stone, being careful to avoid the dragonflies.

"Wow, I've never seen anything like it. I think it glows." Grace cupped the stone in her closed hands and looked at it through the crack between her thumbs.

"Well, it's no fairy, but still it's a pretty cool find. I'll give you that." Jake tossed his stone into the air, watching the trail of light following it, just like the tail of a shooting star. "Awesome, did you see that?"

Julia rubbed her stone across her cheek. "I think it's warm. Is yours warm? Maybe that's why the dragonflies liked them."

The group of dragonflies flew over the fallen tree behind Jake toward the swamp.

"Look where the dragonflies are going. Hey, is that another stone?" Julia pointed to a glimpse of more white. It was in the long grass by the log bridge heading into the swampy area.

Cole moved closer and bent down to pick it up. "It's just a golf ball. Jeeze, I wonder what this is doing here?" Cole tossed the ball over his shoulder. It landed on one of the grassy islands of the swamp.

"I think those are the islands of Never, Never Land." Grace turned to her brother. "Did Mom ever mention stones? Or dragonflies?"

"I don't know but I'm hot. Let's go back and go swimming and we can ask her." Cole tucked his stone into the pocket of his shorts and jumped up.

"It's so awesome that there's one for each of us." Jake

 continued to toss his stone up into the air, mesmerized by the trail of light that it left in its path. "Good thing your cousins aren't here yet, they would definitely want one."

"Yeah, maybe we could find more before they come next week. Cole's right, it's getting hot," Grace agreed, "and I have a new bathing suit that I want to wear. Let's go."

"I guess we could come back tomorrow and check out the swamp," Julia stammered, "maybe that's where the fairies are." She adjusted her glasses, eyes widening, and a smile was creeping onto her face.

The others watched her face light up as she formulated a new idea.

"Or we could find a new adventure idea," she exclaimed, shaking her head vigorously up and down. Then quietly to herself, "Yeah. Yeah, that's what we'll do. We don't need to come back to the swamp." She looked up at Grace. "I can't wait to show you my new suit too. It's got polka dots, and I have this great hair band that goes with it."

"And we can't wait to show you our feet when we beat you to the dock, right Jake?" Cole called as he and Jake took off ahead of the girls again. "See you in the water!"

"What's he talking about, why would we want to see his feet?" Julia crinkled her nose.

Grace laughed. "I think he means when he's swimming in front of us out to the dock. Come on, let's go."

CHAPTER 5
THE DOCK

"Did you guys notice the chipmunks on the way back through the woods?" Julia asked, climbing out of the water onto the floating dock to join the others. "One followed me all the way back to my camp. It was so cute."

"All I saw was Cole's sad eyes when I passed him in the woods. I would have made it to the dock first too, if he hadn't gone straight in the water with his clothes on." Jake grunted and flipped over onto his stomach.

Cole flipped on his stomach too and quickly jumped back up. "Holy smokes, good thing I've got a snap on this pocket. I forgot to take my stone out." He pulled the stone from his pocket. It looked like a pool of oily water, glistening rainbow colors even more brilliantly in the full sun.

"It's beautiful. I hope mine glows like that," Julia gasped, leaning closer to touch the stone. "Maybe it's a real gem."

"I wonder if it glows underwater. Wouldn't it be awesome to dive for it?" Jake asked, leaning over to take the stone from Cole.

"Yo, back off, I have a noodle and I'm not afraid to use it!" Cole cackled in his pirate's voice and swung a yellow noodle around, knocking Jake back and into the water.

Jake surfaced, wiping the water out of his blue eyes. "Fine, dude, you check to see if it glows." The sun's light reflected off the water, making his bristly short hair look blonder and his skin look even darker.

"That's right, I will." Cole threw the noodle with a dramatic twist of his wrist and jumped backward into the water. When he came back to the surface, he held the stone up in triumph. "It glows. This is gonna make for some great diving. But I'm in charge, it's my stone and I don't want to lose it."

"So are you joining us or what?" Jake asked, splashing the girls.

"Definitely," Grace said, jumping into the lake.

Julia climbed down the ladder. "I bet it's even more beautiful underwater."

The kids, all holding their breath, eyes wide open, sunk underwater and watched as Cole held the stone out for them to see. The stone and Cole's hand were sparkling and flickering, pouring beautiful light into the water. They broke back up through the surface, each taking in a deep breath of air.

"That's so cool. It's gonna be wicked easy to find." Jake climbed back up on the dock and got in position to dive. "I'll go first."

"Okay, but you better get it," Cole tossed the stone into the water.

Jake jumped from the dock and quickly surfaced with the stone in hand. "You can totally see it glowing down there. I think I even saw a catfish looking at it."

"I want to try," Grace called, climbing onto the dock.

"Me too, but I don't want to do it alone," Julia said, following Grace up the ladder. "I might not be able to see it without my glasses."

The girls jumped in and came back to the surface with huge smiles.

"That's incredible. Cole, you have to see it. I'll throw it for you this time." Grace panted, treading water.

"I could see it too!" Julia shrieked.

"Awesome, if you can really see it that good, I'm going to let it sink all the way down." Cole stood crouched at the edge of the dock, hands at his sides, ready to dive.

"All right, I'll throw it a little farther out. Here goes." Grace tossed the stone. The trail of light that it left behind made it even more visible and colorful, like the end of a firework on the Fourth of July.

Grace swam back to the dock as Cole's feet disappeared under the surface. All three kids watched on hands and knees.

"Do you see him?" Jake asked.

"No. What's taking so long? I think I see the stone right there." Grace pointed a little to the left.

"Yeah, I see it too, that light right there," Julia agreed. "Look, it's moving."

"There's that catfish again. He must like that stone. But where's Cole? He's totally hogging it," Jake complained.

"Should we go in after him?" Grace asked looking to the left as something caught her eye. "What's with that loon? Is he watching us?"

Just then Cole broke the surface right in front of the kids.

Julia screamed and jumped back in surprise. "Oh thank goodness it's you. I thought you were a giant fish or something."

Cole was up on the dock and already in position, ready to dive again.

"What took so long?" Grace asked. "We were getting scared."

"I don't know. I've got to check something out. Be right back." Cole disappeared under the surface again.

The kids watched. They could see Cole perfectly this time, even as he went deeper, his whole body was glowing with the stone.

"I wonder what he's doing. Look, the catfish is following him, and so is the loon," Jake said, watching Cole swim farther away.

Julia looked toward the shore. "And there's my chipmunk too. See, he's on shore watching us. This is getting a little creepy. Maybe those stones are magical after all," she giggled nervously.

Cole came to the surface again, this time bursting up with the stone in hand, looking like a beam of green light bursting through the blackish, night blue of the mountain lake. The drops of water flying through the air looked like little emeralds, sapphires, and diamonds. "You guys won't believe this. You've got to go get your stones. This is so awesome! Hurry up, go, go, go."

CHAPTER 6
UNDERWATER

"What happened down there?" Jake was the first one back to the dock, stone in hand.

"Wait until the girls get here. You're not gonna believe it. You thought fairies were hard to handle, wait until you hear this." Cole was pacing the dock. "Hurry up, you two!" He called to the girls who were now running into the water, each with a glowing hand.

"So what's the story, what happened down there?" Julia and Grace both asked as they climbed up onto the dock, hands closed around their stones.

"Just hold your stone tight and follow me." Cole jumped into the water and headed toward the bottom, followed by the group of kids and the loon and catfish. He swam around the dock anchor, and led the kids around a fallen tree and a fish hole, a big rock and an old sunken canoe.

The friends stayed together zigging and zagging through the water checking out all the things along the bottom. After a few minutes or so, he headed back to the surface, followed by each of his friends.

"What was that all about? I didn't see anything except the creepy anchor and the weirdo fish and bird following us!" Julia complained. "I tried to keep my eyes on Grace's feet the whole time."

"That was amazing!" Jake yelled and then sunk under the water again.

"Unbelievable! Do you think it's the stone?" Grace asked looking at Cole with giant eyes.

"What? What's unbelievable? What did I miss?" Julia whined, even more upset.

"Yeah, it's got to be the stones. Isn't it the coolest thing ever? We were down there for like five minutes and

Mom doesn't even seem worried. Do you think she just wasn't paying attention?" Grace asked as she and Cole looked toward the beach where their mother was sitting, happily chatting with Julia's mom.

"Oh, she was watching, and so was your mom, Julia. Neither of them seemed to have noticed that we were underwater for so long," Grace said. She looked at Julia, "Didn't *you* notice that we were under there for an unusually long time?"

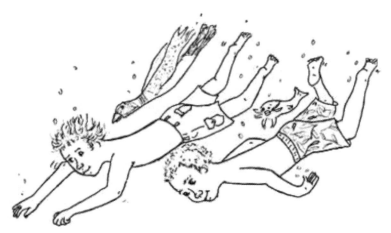

"Well, I guess, but I was concentrating on not being freaked out by the fish and bird and stuff. I guess we were down there a long time." Julia's last words were drawn out, as she finally understood what was so unbelievable. Her eyes were beginning to look like saucers. "Can we breathe underwater?"

Cole shook his head in disbelief. "Yeah, we can. I wonder how it works. Did you notice how much faster you were swimming?" Cole looked into the water as Jake passed under him and came to the surface in the middle of the group.

"Dude, that's the coolest thing ever! I just went over to that dock and back." Jake pointed out across the lake. "How long was I gone? It must have been like ten minutes, right?"

"No, it was like forty-five seconds," Grace said. "That's why our moms didn't notice. Time must be different down there."

Cole looked at Jake, "Are you thinking what I'm thinking? No need for oxygen tanks now. Let's go see the car."

"Oh yeah, now that's what I'm talking about."

"Come on, girls, what do you say?" Cole asked, eyebrows raised.

"NO WAY! It's too dangerous. I'm staying right here." Julia sat down on the dock and crossed her arms and legs.

"I think we were meant to find the stones and go to the car." Grace smiled and gave the boys the thumbs up while sitting down. "But, I think I'll stay here with Julia."

"Well, we'll bring you back the key. My uncle said it's still in the car, and that whoever gets it wins like a million dollars or something." Jake held out his hand, "Agreed?"

Cole threw his hand on top of Jake's. "We'll be rich!"

Grace added her hand to the pile. "Or at least we'll have a key."

Julia slowly stood up and added her hand to the pile, "Just be careful. Maybe the catfish and loon will help you out. Look, I think they would join us if they could." Julia giggled, looking out into the water where the catfish and loon were swimming back and forth in front of the dock.

"One, two, three…" All of the kids raised their hands and shouted together, "CAMP KIDS!"

Jake and Cole looked at each other, looked at the loon and catfish, and dove into the water, holding on tight to their stones.

CHAPTER 7
NEW FRIENDS

Julia and Grace lay on their stomachs on the dock, heads hanging over the edge. They were watching the surface of the water intently, hoping to catch a glimpse of the boys.

"I sure hope those stones work that far down. It will be so neat if they make it all the way to the car." Grace smiled and looked at Julia. "If they make it, then *we'll* definitely have to try too."

"No way, I can hardly think straight with them down there, and I'm getting hungry. How long do you think they will be?"

Both girls looked back into the water.

****

"Whoa, this is totally awesome. Can you hear me, Jake?" Cole yelled, bubbles floating to the surface.

"Yeah, man. No need to yell. I can hear you." Jake put his hand to his mouth, watching the bubbles rise to the surface, as the loon and catfish swam past him to take the lead. "Dude, do you think these two know where we want to go?" Jake asked, pointing ahead to the animals.

"It seems like they're leading us in the right direction. I'm not even getting cold. And it's like we're a giant flashlight. I can see everything."

"Dude, I know. Who would've thought there'd be so many trees down here? And did you see the size of that fish? Maybe it was One-Eyed Willy." Jake loved talking about the legendary One-Eyed Willy, the giant catfish with one eye that his uncle insisted lives in the lake.

The boys continued following the animals, swimming like foreigners lost in a city, looking left and right and up and down. They were mesmerized by the fish swimming by and being able to look up and through the surface at the way the sunlight made stripes in the water. Even the trees surrounding the circular lake looked like a frame on the outside of a mirror, the mirror that they were looking through.

"Hey, did you see that light?" Cole pointed down toward the bottom. "It looked just like the fairies in the woods. Well, I mean like the stones before we knew they were stones."

"Yeah I saw it, and I see you shining too. You look like, well, a fairy too, with no wings of course. Hey, there's another one."

"Wow, you're really glowing too, or shining, I can't tell. You look like the sun reflecting off the lake when it's windy. These stones rule!" Cole turned forward again and continued to swim behind the loon.

"Check it out. I think I see the car. Yeah, it's right there." Jake pointed toward the dark bottom that was getting lighter as the boys swam closer.

"It's just like I thought it would be, straight from Henry Ford." Cole saw the big, old black car.

"No, I thought it would be like a red sports car or something."

"Who would ditch their sports car in the lake?" Cole laughed, a new wave of bubbles escaped from his mouth making him laugh even more. "We must be dreaming or something. This is so cool." Cole held his hand over his mouth and laughed again, watching the bubbles float toward the surface.

"Hey thanks, new friend." Jake waved at the catfish. The catfish turned and waved his tail back at Jake. "Dude, he understands me."

"Thanks to you too, Loony bird. You've been most helpful." Cole bowed to the loon and laughed when the loon dipped his head forward to bow in return. "Unbelievable," he said, shaking his head. He took off swimming and shouted, "Bet I get the key first!"

"NO WAY! My idea, my key!" Jake swam after Cole but ended up crashing into him. "Watch out dude, that's not fair, out of the way!" Jake tried to swim past Cole, but stopped next to him instead, staring ahead, seeing what had made Cole stop so quickly.

Inside of the car were two kids, glowing, just like Jake and Cole. There was a girl about their age with long, white-blond hair sitting in the driver's seat. A sunfish was swimming in and out of her hair. Next to her was a younger

boy with the same light hair and a turtle sitting on his head.

Jake looked at Cole, shrugged his shoulders and said, "Makes as much sense as the rest of this day." He turned to the kids and yelled. "Hi'ya, I'm Jake and this is Cole."

The kids turned and jumped.

The girl broke out in a big smile. "You surprised us! I'm Olivia and this is my brother, Harvey. We're from Brantingham Lake. Where are you from?" She smiled again and swam up and out of the open top of the car toward the boys.

"We're from up there." Jake pointed up to the surface. "How did you get here if you're from Brantingham? Do you have fairy stones?"

"Oh, you must be new at this. Do you mean the star stones? Here they are." Olivia and Harvey both pulled their stones out of the pouches that were hanging around their necks.

"Yeah, we just found ours this morning and decided to see if we could make it to the bottom of the lake. We were heading to this car as a matter of fact," Cole explained.

Harvey's mouth hung open as Cole was talking. "It took us all last summer to figure out that we could breathe underwater with these," he said, holding up a pouch that held his stone. "And you just found them today and you're already down here? You're so lucky!"

"He's right. We just thought that they twinkled at night. We didn't realize until the day before we went home last summer, when Harvey tipped the canoe over, that we could breathe underwater. Luckily he had his star stone pouch on."

"And we've been exploring ever since." Harvey held his chin up. "But you're the first kids that we've seen around here."

"You mean there are more kids with fairy stones? I mean star stones, or whatever you want to call them, with these awesome things?" Cole held up his stone for the others to see.

"Yeah, we met three kids the other day. But we've only explored a few lakes and rivers around here. I think we can go farther, but we haven't tried it yet." Olivia turned to the sunfish and turtle that had been swimming between her and her brother. "We never really know where these guys are going to lead us."

"And I guess that means you two will be leading us on our next adventure?" Jake laughed, looking at the loon and catfish who were both nodding in response.

"How much time goes by when you're down here?" Cole asked. "It's already been like eight minutes. The girls must be freaking out."

"Don't worry, no matter how long you're underwater, no more than a minute goes by above water," Olivia said. "You guys are going to love having these stones. The river channels are so much fun."

"Cool. Is the key still in the car?" Jake asked, thinking only about the infamous prize that his uncle talked about.

"Yeah, it's there." Olivia turned to Harvey. "We'd better get back." She looked back at Cole and Jake. "Leave us a note in the car. Maybe we could show you our lake sometime."

"Cool, sounds great. It was nice meeting you." Cole smiled, only just noticing how beautiful Olivia was, and his words got caught in his throat. "IIIIII hope to ssssee you again tttoo."

Jake grabbed Cole's arm and pulled him toward the car. "See ya. We'll leave you notes and thanks for all the info."

Olivia and Harvey swam away toward what looked like a little tunnel, behind a big rock. They disappeared into it.

"That must be the way to Brantingham. Come on, let's get the key and tell the girls what happened. Bet I get there

first!" Jake turned, swam toward the car, got the key, and took off toward the surface.

The catfish was right in front of him the whole time. Cole and the loon swam right behind.

****

"Don't you hear my stomach growling?" Julia turned again rolling onto her back. "I hope they don't take too long."

Grace jumped up. "Look, there's the loon. It must not have worked, it hasn't been long enough."

The loon popped up through the water just before the boys came blasting through the surface.

"We did it. We made it to the car!" Jake cheered and gave Cole a high five. "Wait till you hear what happened!"

CHAPTER 8
THE KEY

"Where is she already?" Grace asked no one in particular. "I'm going to burst if she doesn't get here soon."

Grace, Cole, and Jake were all sitting around the clubhouse fire pit. Their lunches were spread in front of them on upturned logs that they were using as tables.

"All's I know is that I hope she's packing a good dessert to share. My grandma packed me a hummus and sprout sandwich, cucumber slices, and raisins for dessert. I can't stand this stuff," Jake said, as he took a bite of the sandwich and made a face. "What are sprouts anyway?"

"Sprouts are the shoots off of bean seeds that are soaked and left in a dark place to grow," Grace answered, continuing to look down the dirt road searching for signs of Julia.

"What, do you have an encyclopedia in your head or something? I wasn't really expecting an answer, you know." Jake put his sandwich back in the baggie and picked up the cucumber slices. "At least I know what these are."

Cole laughed as Jake took an exaggerated bite of the cucumber, acting like it was a delicacy, licking his fingertips after each tiny nibble.

"Hey, wait for me!" Julia called, coming around the side of a camp, into view of the clubhouse. She was carrying a small cooler and a picnic basket.

"Hurry up, I can't wait any longer!" Grace called out.

Julia began to run, all of her lunch gear banging into her legs with each step. Her glasses were already sliding down her small nose, her hair ribbon was back in place, and her new chipmunk friend was scampering behind.

She arrived to the circle out of breath, dropped the cooler and opened the picnic basket as she sat on her log. "All right, let me just get my lunch out and then tell us everything. Come on, Chippy, find a seat." Grace patted her lap and the chipmunk climbed up.

"Just start talking, boys." Grace nodded to the boys then looked at Julia. "You can listen and unpack at the same time. Cute name, by the way. I take it you're friendly," Grace said, stroking Chippy's head. She sat down and looked at the boys, pencil and journal ready.

"So, it was the coolest thing. The loon got right in front of me and the catfish swam right in front of Jake. It was like they knew right where we were going and they led us straight to the car." Cole's eyes got bigger with each word.

"Yeah, and then we saw these two kids sitting in the car, and we were like 'Well, I guess that's no weirder than the rest of this day.' So, Jake calls out to them and then we like chatted for a while and got the key and here we are." Jake smiled, knowing he was driving Grace crazy, skipping so much of the story.

"Come on, stop messing around. We're dying here. Tell us everything. Did you say *kids*?" Grace was nearly shaking with frustration.

"All right here it is."

Cole and Jake told the girls every last detail. Grace filled all the rest of the pages in her summer journal. She was just closing it and picking up her sandwich when she realized that they hadn't even seen the key yet.

"Where is the…" Grace began, but Jake had started talking at the same time.

"Here it is." He reached into his pocket and tried to pull out the key, but the key chain got stuck. He fiddled with it a bit more and then yanked it out. "Yes, here it is, and I'm the one who got it!"

"It looks like one of those old house keys. Not a car key," Grace thought out loud.

"Yeah it's a skeleton key, like the one we have for the barn at home." Cole reached over and ran his thumb down the edge of the key.

"The key to our camp looks just like that." Julia mumbled through a mouthful of potato chips.

"Can I see it?" Grace asked, taking the key from Jake. "What do you think this is?" Hanging from the key was a carved piece of wood. It was old, water worn, and broken.

"It kinda looks like a moose. Hey, that could mean." Cole didn't finish the sentence, but looked at the door of the clubhouse.

"It could be that moose. It's the right size and everything, just missing an antler." Jake walked over to the cabin and touched the moose that he had touched that morning when he raced Cole to the clubhouse. Who knew then, that this day, this very first day of summer, would be the adventure of a lifetime?

Cole, Grace, and Julia were right behind Jake looking at the moose above the keyhole. Chippy had settled down to eat the remains of Julia's sandwich, while watching the children.

"All right, here goes nothing." Grace put it into the keyhole. It slid right in and turned easily.

Jake grabbed the door handle. "On three, let's all go in together: one, two, three."

All four kids pushed on the door, but it wouldn't budge.

"You've got to be kidding. After all that and it doesn't work?" Cole groaned, shoulders slumped.

"Wait, you didn't put the moose in, silly." Julia reached for the key chain and put the moose in the cutout on the door. It fit perfectly. She turned the door handle and the door to the clubhouse swung open.

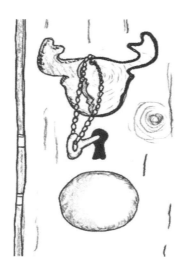

CHAPTER 9
INSIDE, AT LAST

"How did you know you had to put the moose in the door?" Cole and Grace asked at the same time.

"I don't know, I guess I just knew." Julia pushed up her glasses and walked into the cabin behind Grace and the boys.

Inside, there was a big stone fireplace with a thick wood mantel. It was covered with little rocks. Above the mantel was an oil painting of an underwater scene. A large paned window was opposite the fireplace. The drapes that looked so dark from outside were almost translucent from inside.

The walls were thick logs, with shelves cut out here and there, with more little gray rocks sitting on them. There were four chairs all positioned in a circle around a big tree-stump table. On the table there were maps and binoculars and compasses, and books about mythical creatures, and journals (including what looked to be waterproof ones).

"Whoa, look at all this stuff," Jake said, picking up one of the books about mythical creatures.

Grace headed for the journals stacked on the table. Julia wandered around looking at all of the things pinned to the walls. Cole began sifting through the pile of maps sitting on the table.

"It's like it was here just waiting for us." Grace flipped open the top journal and began reading.

"No kidding, these maps are awesome. They're of lakes and rivers all over the world. Well, they're actually maps of the bottoms of the lakes and rivers. You've got to see this." Cole passed one of the maps to Jake.

Jake was so engrossed in the mythical creatures book that he was reading, that Cole had to hit him with the map to get his attention.

"What? Why are you hitting me?" Jake didn't look up and didn't wait for an answer. "You've got to see these books. They talk about all sorts of mythical water creatures around the world, including some right here in the Adirondacks. Check it out." He looked up and handed Cole the book. He took the map from Cole's outstretched hand. "What's this?"

"Just take a look," Cole insisted as he handed Jake the map and flipped open the book.

Julia stood behind Cole, looking over his shoulder as he turned the pages. She was tossing one of the rocks that she had picked up from the mantle. Nobody spoke for a minute or two, each child thinking about what they were seeing and how this day seemed so unreal.

"Hey, you guys," Grace exclaimed. "Listen, you've got to hear this." She cleared her throat and read from the journal:

If you are reading this, then you are now a water sprite. You have been chosen to become a part of the water world. You will learn more about your new powers in the books on the table.

You must always be careful. Sprites have been able to survive in the Adirondacks for thousands of years, but they, and now you, need the help of the woodland and water animals to guide you and warn you of danger.

One day your stone will not work anymore, so honor the underwater world by respecting your powers and using the magic of the stone to improve the lives of the sprites, animals, and waters of the world.

"And check out who signed it. That's Mom and Auntie Lorraine and Auntie Marie and Uncle Kevin. And isn't that your mom and your aunt and uncle, Julia?" Grace pointed to the names Kimmy, MaryAnn and Tim. "And isn't that your mom, Jake? Look right there: Linda."

"Yeah," Jake whispered. He kept staring at the names.

Julia fiddled with the stone in her hand. "Oh my gosh, you guys. Look, this is my mom's stone. Her name's right here and there's a picture of a deer. That must have been her animal guide." Julia had a tear welling in her eye. "Does that really mean that we are all water sprites, whatever they are? And that my mom is one too? Why wouldn't she say anything?"

"She couldn't and we can't either." Grace looked back down at the journal. "It says that we shouldn't tell anyone and that when we are too old to use the magic uninhibited, the stone won't work and we won't remember being a sprite."

"Uninhibited? What does that mean?" Julia asked while looking at her own stone. "Hey, look it's Chippy." Julia showed Grace the etched picture of a chipmunk under her name in her stone.

Grace smiled and looked at her stone. She turned to Cole. "Can I see your stone?"

Cole tossed her his stone and continued to look at the mythical creatures book. Grace saw his name and a picture of a loon etched carefully in its sparkly surface. She tossed it back to Cole. She stood up and walked over to look at Jake's stone. She clearly saw his name and a picture of a catfish.

She looked at her own again. Grace was written clear as day, but etched underneath her name were just two eyes, no animal. What on earth could that mean? What was her animal guide? Everyone else, even Olivia and Harvey knew their guides. She shook her head and figured maybe she could find out in one of the books on the table, but first things first.

"Let's find out what water sprites are. Did you guys see them in that book?" Grace picked up three more mythical creatures books and handed one each to Jake and Julia.

"No, I didn't see one yet," Jake snapped, snatching the book from her hand.

"Okay, sorry." Grace just stared at Jake, trying to figure out what had made him so mad.

"Here they are." Cole turned his book so everyone could see.

The picture in the book showed tiny humanlike glowing creatures sitting on rocks beside the water. The picture was in black and white, but it was clear that the creatures were twinkling and glowing, just like the kids had in the water.

"But we don't look like that," Julia sighed.

Grace shook her head. "No, but remember, the people writing these books and drawing these pictures probably only heard about the sprites, or just caught a glimpse of one once and made up the rest. Look what it says: 'Water sprites are childlike water dwelling creatures found in all parts of history all over the world. It is believed that they are travelers, never staying in one place long.' That sounds just like what I think we can do."

The kids continued reading the books and journals and exploring the room until it started to get dark. Their parents would be calling for them soon. The first day of summer at camp was nearly over.

"I say we go here first." Jake pointed to a picture of the Mediterranean Sea, showing mermaids hanging off boats. "What do you say Cole?" he asked through gritted teeth and a forced smile. He could not believe that Mom had managed to work her way into his thoughts today. She did not deserve any of his attention. He hadn't thought about her all day until now. Had she really been a sprite?

"What about here?" Cole said without looking up. He pointed to a picture of Scotland and Loch Ness, with Nessy's blurry head poking out of the water.

"No, let's go here." Julia held up a picture of the liquid streets of Venice where there was a Chimaira, part serpent, goat, and another unidentifiable creature part. "I love Italian food."

"Or, since we are all new at this, maybe we should go here." Grace held her book, *Little Known Creatures of the Adirondacks*, up for the group to see. It had a black and white photograph of a group of glowing children sitting on a sunken ship. The photo was taped to the back cover. It had a hand-written caption which read, "Our favorite spot, Brantingham Lake, summer 1954."

"It's settled then. Tomorrow morning we'll meet at the beach and go exploring. Who knows, maybe Harvey and Olivia will be waiting at the car." Grace put her hand in.

Cole, Jake, and Julia placed their hands on top of Grace's. They counted to three and without talking about it first, the kids all shouted "Water Sprites!"

CHAPTER 10
TO THE NEXT LAKE

"I'm here. Let's make a plan before our dad gets down here." Cole plopped down next to Jake and watched as Grace worked on re-creating the map of Brantingham Lake in the sand.

After trying for the last two days to make it to the ship, Grace had decided to tack the map to the wall of the bedroom she and Cole shared. They just couldn't figure out how Olivia and Harvey made it into the river channel.

"I'm really hoping that they've left us a note in the car," Grace said as she finished drawing an "X" to mark the spot where they would find the ship.

Grace had left a note, zipped in a plastic baggie, hoping that Olivia and Harvey would come back and see it.

"Me, too, I don't want to get caught in that current again." Julia pushed her glasses up and took a bite of her cinnamon roll.

"Hey, give me some of that," Jake demanded, putting his hand out for a piece. "I had a wheat germ and yogurt shake for breakfast. I swear if it weren't for you Julia, I would've lost ten pounds already this summer. I think my grandparents might be trying to kill me."

"Yesterday, Loony and the catfish kept swimming over toward that rock." Cole drew a picture of a rock on the sand map at the end of the river channel leading to Brantingham Lake. "I think that must have something to do with getting through the current. I'm sure if we follow their lead, we'll figure it out today."

"I bet you're right. We probably need to move the rock somehow." Grace made a note in her journal.

"That's a great idea, but that rock is enormous. I know Cole and I are hugely muscular, and I may be the best player on my football team, but I think there are limits to our strength." Jake held up his arms, flexing his muscles for the girls to see.

"Look, there's Dad. Let's just go check it out," Grace said, ignoring Jake and dusting the sand map away with her foot. "Can we go in, Dad?"

Mr. Galley was holding a cup of coffee and a newspaper. Even if time did pass when they were underwater, he would never notice with his nose in the paper the whole time.

"Sure, just watch out for the sea monster," Mr. Galley laughed, pointing to a picture in the newspaper, showing the blurry long neck of something coming out of the water.

"Yeah, okay Dad," Cole said, shrugging his shoulders turning and rolling his eyes to his friends. "Beat you to the Dock!" Cole pushed past Jake's still flexed arm and ran into lake.

Grace, Jake, and Julia (in her new purple prescription goggles that her mom bought for her after much begging), all ran in after him. Their skin was twinkling, blending into the morning reflection on the lake as they swam easily to the dock. The loon and the catfish were at the front of the group. Chippy watched from the water's edge.

Cole was the first to the dock but he was quickly greeted with Jake's favorite song. "First is the worst, second is the best, third is the one with the hairy chest! Sorry Gracey, but you're going to look like an ape by the end of summer!" Jake laughed hard at his own joke, slapping his knee in exaggeration.

Ignoring Jake, Grace looked at her brother, "Cole, you'd better go first, it seems like Loony always takes the lead anyway." She smirked at Jake, sticking up for her brother's position in first. "Let's go to the car and see if there's a note."

Cole gave Grace the thumbs up and dove into the water following the loon, the rest of the camp kids followed like a shimmering line of silver fish.

CHAPTER 11
CHANNELS

The kids swam to the car. Jake sat in the back, looking over the seat. The other kids were gathered around the glove box, waiting for Grace to open it.

It had only been a few days that they had been water sprites, but it felt so natural now. The sheer amazement of being able to breathe underwater no longer captivated their every thought.

Well, for everyone except Julia, who eyes were so wide that it looked like her goggles were made of magnifying glasses. She was always on the lookout for scary fish, and scary pine needles, and scary old boots.

"Perfect, they left a note," Grace said, picking up two waxy notebooks that were lying in the glove box. She opened the one labeled "Car Journal". "Here, I'll read it." Grace cleared her throat and began to read:

Tink (Harvey's turtle) always sits next to the big rock. Maybe he's changing the current. Good Luck! Leave us notes in one of the waterproof journals, and the other is a gift to you (they're from our grandma-cool huh?).

Olivia and Harvey

"It's just like we thought, I bet the turtle is blocking the spring that makes the current," Cole said, taking the note from Grace. "I'll just write back to say thanks."

"What are you doing? Writing a love note?" Jake teased. "I saw how you looked at Olivia when we met her."

"Oh, give it up, Jake. I'm just writing back, I hardly noticed how pretty she was." Cole's round cheeks turned pink. He quickly turned his head and began writing again.

"Enough boys, I really want to make it through the river channel today." Grace took the notebook from Cole and put it back in the glove box. "Come on, let's get going."

The kids could see everything clearly. As long as they had their fairy stones, their own glowing skin would light the water, as bright as a summer's day above water. Cole spotted the river channel and the big boulder and slowed down, waiting for his friends to catch up.

"Jake, you and Julia get ready to try and go in the river channel. Grace and I will try to figure out where to put this rock to change the current." Cole bent down and picked up a turtle- sized rock that was on the sandy ground.

"It looks like it's the perfect size. Julia, get ready, when the current stops, hold on 'cause we're going though!" Jake took Julia's hand and struggled against the current to get as close to the river channel opening as he could.

Julia screamed and clung to Jake's arm. The current pushed her straight hair from her face, her fairy stone pouch was flying behind her and her new goggles perfectly framed her wide open, dark brown eyes. She looked petrified.

"Julia, loosen your grip! You're gonna rip my arm off." Jake turned to yell more, but he saw the look on her face. "Chill out, we'll be fine." He turned back and shouted to Cole and Grace. "We're ready!"

They could barely hear him over the current.

"Look, put it here, in this clear area." Grace heard Julia scream again. "Quick Cole, put it down before Julia loses her nerve."

Cole struggled to put the small rock over the cleared area, but there was a force pushing it away. "Help me, Grace, it's too hard!"

Grace swam over and helped Cole to push on the rock, but it was like trying to push the opposite ends of a magnet together. They just couldn't get the rock to the ground.

"Come on, Loony, help us out, what are we supposed to do?" Cole yelled to the loon that had been watching the kids struggle.

As though he had been waiting for an invitation, he swam over and sat on top of the rock. The rock immediately fell to the ground. The loon winked at the kids.

"I guess we just needed to ask. Sorry, Loony, I forgot you know all this stuff." Cole stroked the loon's head.

"Wow, good work, Loony. That definitely stopped the current, the water is perfectly still," Grace said as she turned to look at the river channel opening. The big rock had moved slightly exposing a dark tunnel. Jake and Julia were gone. She opened the new waterproof journal to make some notes.

"Don't do that now. Come on. Let's see what's on the other side." Cole took Grace's hand and they swam together into the river channel.

As soon as they entered the channel, they felt the current against them again. Loony quickly led them to the bottom where the current changed, helping to push them forward instead of pulling them back. It was so strong that they were pushed through the channel and spit out the other end before they could even look around to see what it was like inside.

Cole and Grace flew out of the tunnel, turning circles and twisting over each other. Jake and Julia, already recovered from their own tumbling exit from the channel, giggled while they watched their friends try to figure out which way was up.

"That was awesome!" Cole said, finally making it to his feet. He looked at Loony who was walking crooked, dizzy after turning somersaults in the channel. "Are you all right?"

The loon looked up at his friend, smiled, and fell over onto his back shaking in what appeared to be giggles.

"I think he likes it." Grace began laughing too. "It was like riding a waterslide with no gravity, like we're at a water park on the moon."

"When I was done being scared and opened my eyes, it was all over," Julia moaned. "I wish I would just relax."

"Yeah, me too," Jake complained, rubbing his red arms, which had very distinct imprints from Julia's fingers. "You've got to chill like me and my cool catfish!"

"Oops, sorry Jake." Julia giggled now, watching Jake nurse
his arm.

"Oh stop complaining you two, we finally made it. Let's go exploring." Cole looked at Jake. "I bet I can spot more bass than you can on the way to the ship."

"No way, I've got Coolcat to help me." Jake looked down at his catfish. "It's a perfect name for you, huh?" The catfish stood on his hind fins and nodded in agreement. Jake looked at Grace. "How do we get there anyway?"

She had the new journal open and was drawing the map on the first page. "Follow me, I know the way!" Grace swam off, grabbing Julia's hand as she went. "You can stick with me, Julia."

CHAPTER 12
CURRENTS

The line of silvery, flickering water sprites again swam together through the water. Every once in a while, Grace would stop to record the new plants that she saw and draw pictures of the new fish.

They had seen bass, perch, sunfish, bullheads, minnows, frogs, turtles, and ducks. In the big lake there were new things to worry about, and Loony and Coolcat were very helpful.

"Watch out, dude!" Jake yelled to the other kids. A wave hit them before they even heard the warning. Another motorboat passed overhead and caused the water around them to push at them in waves, just like above water.

"I'm starting to feel seasick," Julia held her stomach, "or maybe I'm just getting hungry."

"It does take a little getting used to." Grace was having a hard time keeping the journal open, each wave flipping the pages like the wind might. "Oh forget it, I will write all this later." She stopped to slide the journal on the string of her fairy stone pouch and then swam to catch up with the boys.

Julia, who had stopped with Grace, bent down to check out a "scary" boot that was at the bottom of the lake. A frog was sitting in it.

"Hey, Hoppy, how's it going?"

The frog looked up at Julia and winked his big eye at

 her, then waved his long fingers. Julia smiled and waved back. The frog looked off into the distance and kept waving.

Julia turned to see what he was waving at and realized that Grace was gone. Julia could just see her, disappearing around the edge of an island.

She was alone. She swam as fast as she could toward the island, but without Loony and Coolcat's warnings, she didn't feel the current pulling at her until it was too late. It took her whole body and pulled her back, right toward the island, as if a rug had been pulled out from underneath her. She could only catch glimpses of the land as she tumbled. She was being tossed around and around.

Then, she saw it, a river channel, looking like a big black cave. She was flowing with the current right into it, and it was not the river channel leading to her lake. Quickly she began to swim perpendicular to the current, like she had been taught when she went to Cape Cod one summer. It slowed her down enough to see the big, black hole getting closer, but not enough to stop her being taken right into it.

Julia shut her eyes and screamed, terrified of what was going to happen next. She knew when her body entered the tunnel. It was dead silent and it felt like she was being sucked head first through a straw. The current pulled with such force that she wouldn't have been able to open her eyes if she tried.

CHAPTER 13
JULIA

"Oh my, oh my, oh my." Julia lay face down on the sandy lake bottom, right where she was set down by the channel current. "Okay, Julia, you can do it. Just open one eye."

She had been trying to convince herself that she was really just dreaming and lying in her own bed at camp. All she had to do now was open her eyes and see the posters lining her ceiling. She lifted her head and squinted through one eye.

"No posters? I'm not dreaming? That means that I'm lost, underwater, by myself? Okay, Julia, don't panic. Right, all I need to do is go back. The river channel should be right behind me."

She turned.

"Oh great, that's just great. Two channels right next to each other? But I don't know which one is the right one."

She dropped to her knees and a stream of thoughts ran through her head.

"I'm never going to Paris. I'll never try caviar or truffles. I'm never going to have a five-tiered wedding cake, never going to meet my prince charming, or get a puppy, or get the pink polar bear that I ordered, or use that cool torch to make that yummy French desert, or, or see my parents again."

She held her head in her hands and began sobbing uncontrollably. Bubbles were floating everywhere. She was shaking up and down.

Then, she heard a noise. Was that voices?

She looked up, just in time to see two blond-haired kids being shot out of one of the river channels, landing right at her feet.

They were riding the current like they were on surf boards, smiles on their faces, whooping and hollering with pure joy.

"Oh sorry, were you trying to get through to Big Moose Lake?" the beautiful girl asked.

Julia was still so stunned that she couldn't even think clearly enough to answer. She just stared at the kids, mouth open, waiting for the words to find their way out with the bubbles.

"Are you all right?" the girl asked, coming closer.

Her white-blond hair was flowing behind her like a silky blanket, her green eyes matched the color of her bathing suit, and her bathing suit matched the color of the water. She just needed a tail and she would look just like a mermaid from one of the books at the clubhouse. A sunfish swam around her, catching the light like a moving rainbow, making the girl even more beautiful.

The boy looked like a short-haired match to the older girl, same light hair and green eyes. He swam over to Julia and looked her right in the eye.

"Olivia, I think she must be one of Jake and Cole's friends. I bet she got caught in the river channel current like I did last week." Harvey leaned closer, looking deeper into

Julia's eyes. "Are Jake and Cole here too?" he asked her, setting the turtle that he had been holding down on the ground.

Julia shook her head side to side. "The ship." She took a deep breath, finally finding her words and began rambling, "We were going to the ship and I stopped to see a cute frog, and the next thing I knew I was caught in this current and I'm here all by myself, and I don't even know where I am."

"It's a good thing we came when we did." Olivia reached down to take Julia's arm and help her up. "You're okay now. We'll take you back to Brantingham and to the ship to find your friends. You must have been so scared."

"You saved my life." Julia hugged Olivia and then Harvey. "I'm going to bake you the best cookies ever. And I am never going to swim again. Never!"

"Oh, that's too bad. Harvey and I were planning to invite you and your friends to see a sunken boat that we found."

"Well, you will just have to tell me about it because I am never swimming again. I might just write the river channel company. Who do you think made these things anyway?" Julia held her fairy stone and continued talking. "I just kept thinking how my mom would be all alone without me if I had been lost at sea. If I was eaten by a shark, she would never even know. What would she tell my dad when he brings me a new game this weekend? Would he return it? Or would he play it, or worst of all give it away? What if I never got to wear diamonds? Hey do you think there is a treasure in that sunken boat? And what if…?

Olivia took her hand and the three kids swam together into the river channel. Julia continued talking the whole time.

CHAPTER 14
CAMP KIDS AGAIN

"I am *so* happy to see you. I was so scared that I would end up in the Amazon or something and then I would be eaten by piranhas and I would never see my parents again." Julia took all of her friends, who had been frantically searching the lake, into a big hug.

Then she turned and hugged Harvey and Olivia. "These two saved my life. I owe them everything. Oh and by the way, I am never swimming again. Well, unless there is a treasure in that boat they found."

"Actually, we found her in the Chain Lakes. We've been having a great time checking out all the river channels leading to other small lakes. We could show you," Olivia offered, looking directly at Cole.

"Awesome, let's go." Cole was so swept up listening to Olivia that he forgot about how upset Julia was.

"Cole, I want to go home. I want to be on land, and I want to see my mom. I almost died out there." Julia hung her head and held the wooden deer that her mom had given her. It was hanging on her fairy stone pouch string.

"Yeah, you're right, I'm sorry." Cole quickly recovered from the mesmerizing spell that he seemed to fall under when he saw Olivia.

Grace took Julia's hand. "I won't let go the whole way back, I promise. You must have been so scared." She turned to Olivia. "I'm Grace. The boys told us all about you. Thanks for the note and for the notebook, and for saving Julia." Grace put her hand on the notebook and hugged her friend.

Cole looked around at all of his glowing friends, their hair floating above them, and their skin glistening; the loon, catfish, sunfish, and turtle all watching and listening to the plans. "We could meet back here tomorrow and we could all go to the Chain Lakes together."

"I have a tennis lesson tomorrow," all three girls said at the same time. They laughed and began their own conversation about meeting up at the club for tennis.

The boys gathered together to make their plans. "I'm free, how about you? Want to meet tomorrow?" Jake asked, making a plan with Cole and Harvey to meet the next morning.

The camp kids said good-bye to their sprite friends and swam off toward the river channel that would lead them back to their lake. Julia held on to Grace's hand extra tight when they rounded the corner of the island. The journey back through to their small lake was much easier and more fun, now that they knew what to expect.

When they arrived back at the dock, Mr. Galley was still reading the newspaper and drinking his morning coffee. The kids climbed out of the water, exhausted.

They all rested back on the dock, the sun warming them, listening to Julia tell about her harrowing experience. They talked about the new friends and the new things to look out for in the river channels and bigger lakes. They planned to meet up at the clubhouse later in the day and read through the maps of the Chain Lakes while they waited for Grace and Cole's cousins to arrive. And they argued over which camp would have the best fireworks display.

Grace stood up, now hot and dry. "How about a game of Tag Around the Dock?" She put her hand out.

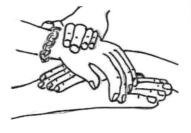

"Well, I said I would never swim again, but I do like Tag Around the Dock. Oh, okay." Julia stood and placed her hand on top of Grace's.

"Get ready to lose!" Jake said getting up and sliding his hand under the pile.

"Oh, I'm ready to watch *you* lose!" Cole laughed and snuck his hand under Jake's.

"Yep, you guys never change. One, two, three…Camp Kids!"

Each of the children fell exhausted into bed that night.

Their dreams were full of visions of their adventures so far and of the adventures still to come. For Cole it was challenges, for Julia fear, for Grace it was knowledge, and for Jake excitement.

Together these water sprites would find all of these things, that summer and for many more summers, in their new underwater world.

For this was only the beginning.

also available:

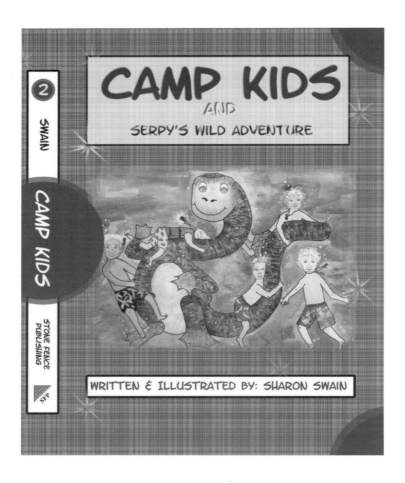

Look for it at
www.campkidsbooks.com